To my grandchildren Liam, Maddy, Kate, Teddy, Abby, Hunter and, especially, Eva who inspired me to write this book.

So Big Yet So Small

PRT0614D

Printed in the United States

ISBN-13: 978-1-937406-16-5
ISBN-10: 1-937406-16-4

www.mascotbooks.com

So BIG
Yet So Small

Peter Weiland

Illustrated by Kevin Coffey

Hello. I'm an aircraft carrier. I'm very, very big. I'm also very, very small. How is that possible? To be very big and very small at the same time? Read on and you'll find out.

But first, what is an aircraft carrier? It is a ship that carries aircraft. It has a long, flat deck that goes from one end of the ship to the other. That is why it is sometimes called a "Flat Top." Airplanes can take off from this long deck, called the flight deck, and also land on it. So it is a very unusual ship.

Can you run all the way from one soccer goal to the one at the other end of the field? It's hard. But an aircraft carrier is as long as three soccer fields. To run from one end of the flight deck of an aircraft carrier to the other end would be like running from the soccer goal at one end of the field to the one at the other end, then back to the first one and then back again to the other. Phew! That's really big isn't it?

So that's how long an aircraft carrier is. But it is also big up and down. There are about six decks down on the ship and six decks up. That's like a big hotel or apartment building. To go from the bottom of the ship to the top is like climbing twelve stories. Your home probably has two or three stories. An aircraft carrier has twelve. And if you want to go up or down you don't use an elevator. You climb from one floor to another on ladders. They are steep and narrow. You would get very tired if you had to climb from the bottom of the ship all the way to the tippy top.

How many people do you think live on an aircraft carrier? Over five thousand. Imagine! It is like a small city. It has a big cafeteria (we call it a mess deck) where the cooks prepare three meals a day for five thousand people. It is a very big restaurant. When your Mommy makes soup for you she does it in a pot on the stove and stirs it with a spoon. When the cook on an aircraft carrier makes soup for 5,000 sailors he does it in a pot as tall as you and the stirrer he uses is like the oar from a rowboat.

Because an aircraft carrier is like a small city it also has a laundry to wash the crews' clothes and a dry cleaning shop to clean their dress uniforms.

It has a small hospital with doctors to treat people who get sick.

It has a dentist and a dentist's chair and a barber and a barber's chair.

It has a jail, called a brig, in case any crewmember misbehaves and breaks the rules.

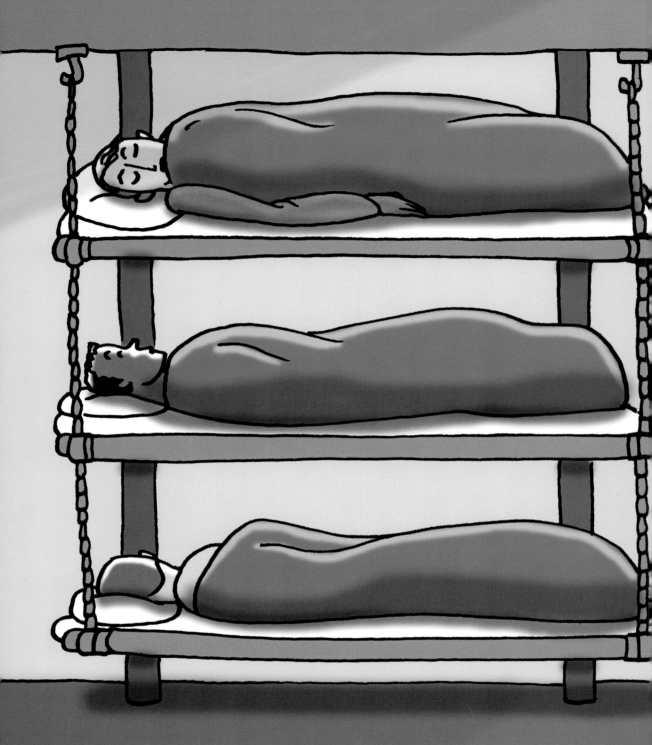

Where do all these people sleep? The ship has many bedrooms. But the beds aren't nice, comfy beds like you have at home. Do you know what a bunk bed is? The sailors sleep in bunk beds but there aren't just

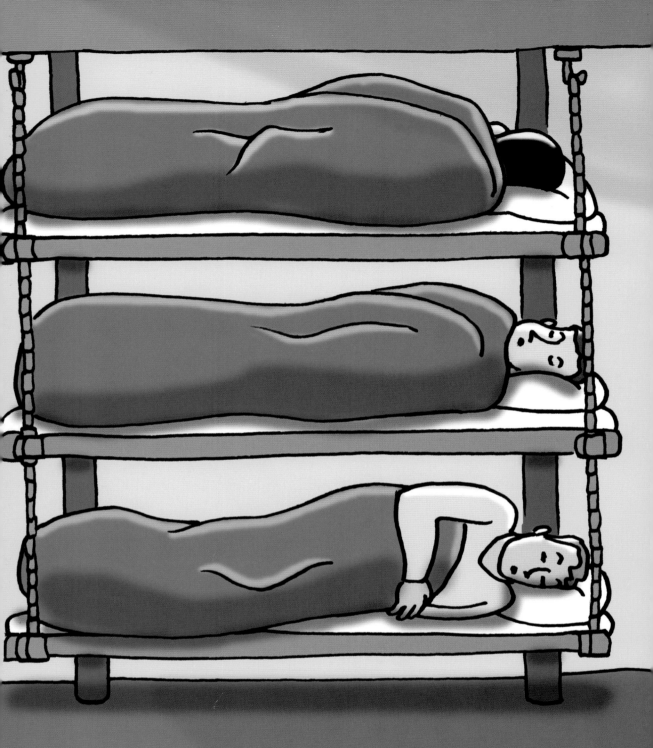

two bunks, one on top of the other, there are three and there are often 60 sailors in one bunk room. The quarters are close and people must learn to get along with each other.

Finally, the aircraft carrier has a geedunk. A geedunk is like an ice cream parlor.

So if a sailor has some time off he can go to the geedunk and get an ice cream cone.

An aircraft carrier, like me, is so big that it often cannot fit alongside a dock. So when I go into a port sometimes I anchor out. That is, when I go into the harbor I drop my anchor and then lower small boats into the water to take the sailors to and from the dock. Do you know how much my anchor weighs? Twelve tons. That's as much as six big cars all squished together. And the chain that holds the anchor......Does your Mommy have a gold chain with a little pendant that she wears around her neck sometimes? The links are tiny aren't they? But the links in the chain that holds the anchor are huge. Each one weighs as much as two of you. That anchor and chain are what holds the ship still so I don't drift away with the tide.

So that's how big, how very big, an aircraft carrier is.

Now I'll show you how small it is.

When you get in an airplane with your Mom and Dad to go visit your Grandma or go on vacation, do you look out the window? If you do you will see that as the plane turns onto the runway just before

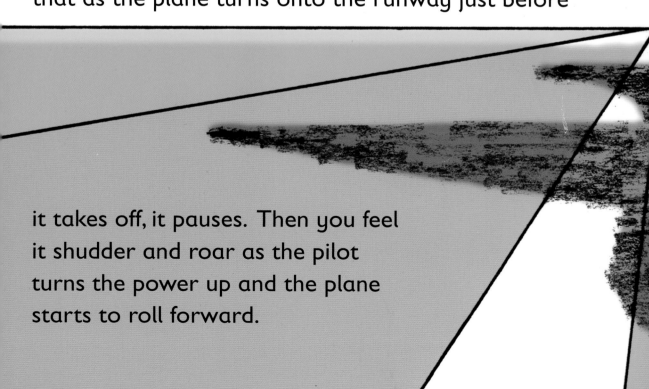

it takes off, it pauses. Then you feel it shudder and roar as the pilot turns the power up and the plane starts to roll forward.

Faster and faster it goes - thumpity, thumpity, thump! Finally it starts to rise, the thumping stops and the ride becomes smooth. The plane has taken off. To do this it had to roll along a runway,

gradually increasing its speed until it was flying. The runway, which is like a wide concrete road, is over two miles long. A lot longer than an aircraft carrier.

Same thing when you're landing. You look out the window and see the plane getting closer and closer to the ground. Finally it touches down and you hear a roar as the pilot puts on the brakes and slows the plane down until finally it stops and then turns off the runway. It took the plane a long time to come to a stop on the two mile long runway.

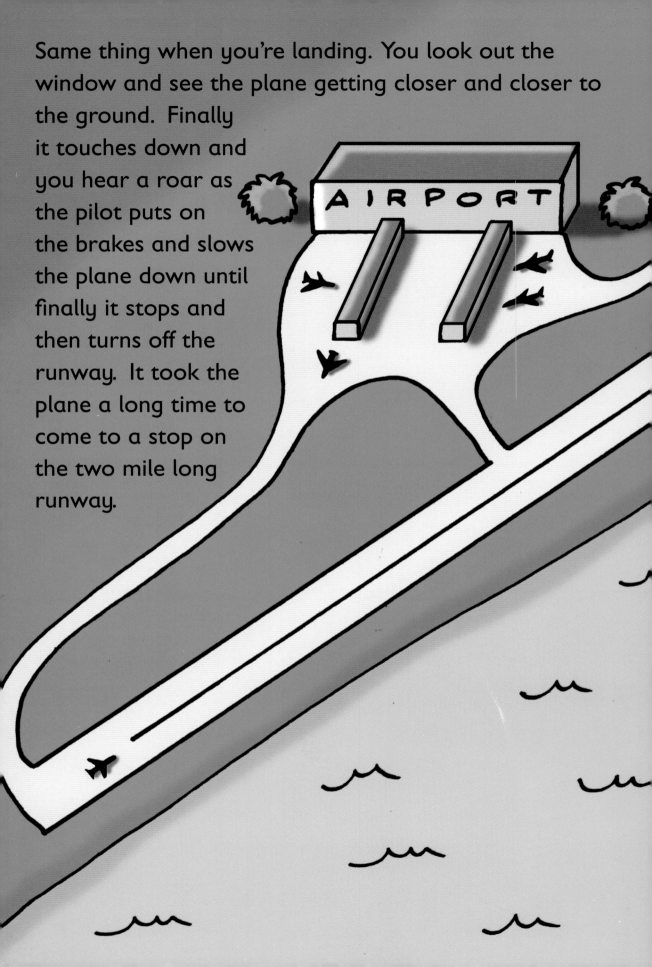

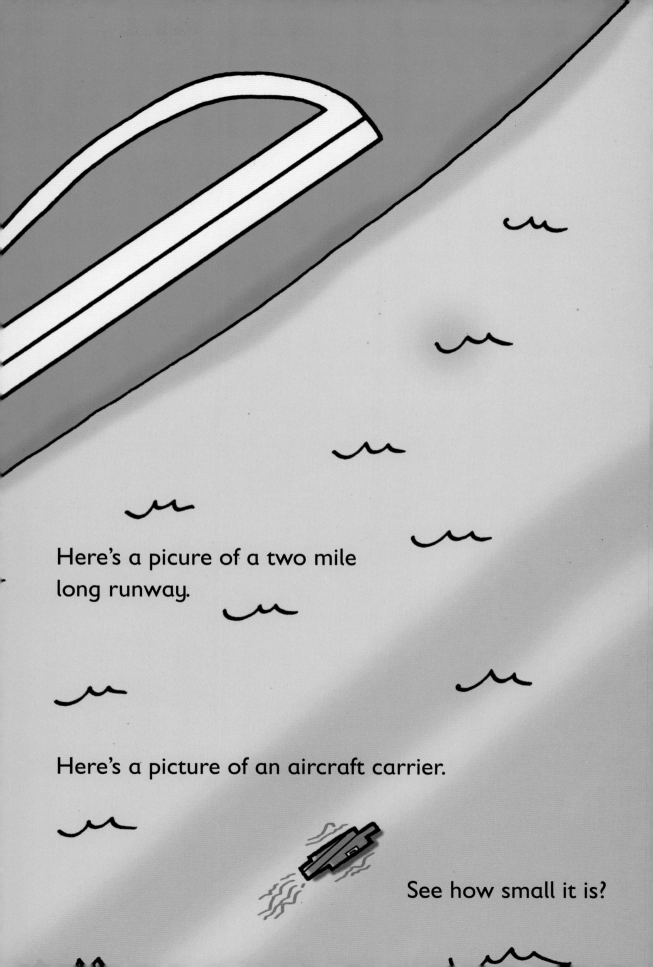

Here's a picure of a two mile long runway.

Here's a picture of an aircraft carrier.

See how small it is?

So how does a pilot take off from a runway that is as small as an aircraft carrier? The answer is a catapult. A catapult is like a big slingshot. Do you know what a slingshot is? No? Here's one.

An aircraft carrier has four giant catapults.
They accelerate a plane from zero to one
hundred and fifty miles per hour in less than
two seconds. They literally shoot the plane
into flight.

And how does a pilot land a plane on an aircraft carrier? It is much too short to allow the landing plane to roll along and finally come to a stop. Each Navy plane has attached to its fuselage a tailhook. This is a ten foot long steel bar with a hook on the end. When the plane is flying the bar and hook are nestled tight against the fuselage.

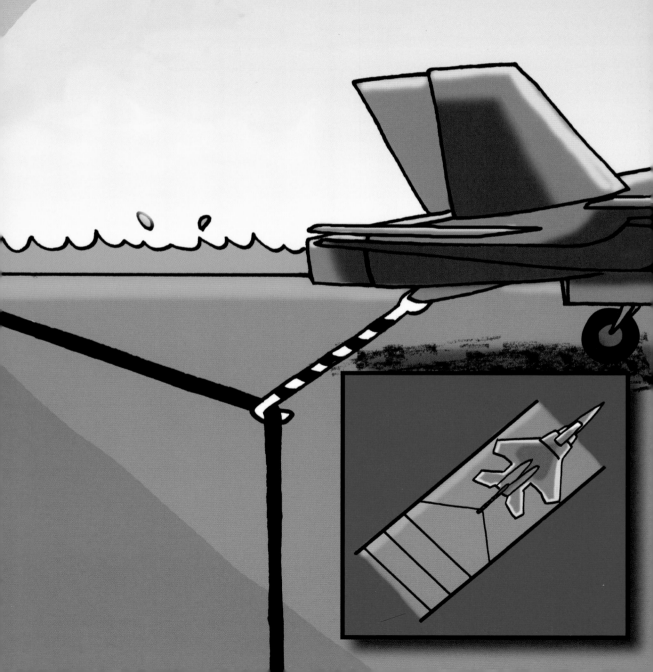

When the pilot is ready to land, he pushes a lever in the cockpit and the hook end of the bar rotates and extends down. The ship, in the meantime, has strung four wire cables across the flight deck. Each one is spring loaded. The pilot lands and the hook catches one of the four wires and the plane comes to a halt - not in two miles but in 400 feet and in less than two seconds.

So that is how a pilot takes off from and lands on a huge ship which is very small when compared to an airport runway.

See, an aircraft carrier is very,
very big and, also...

very, very small. All at the same time.

Pete Weiland is a former Naval Aviator
who flew AD-5W Skyraiders with Carrier
Airborne Early Warning Squadron 12 in
the 1950s. He deployed on board the USS
Intrepid on which he recorded 100 landings
including 22 night landings. Pete and his wife,
Mary Rose, reside near Princeton, New Jersey.
Retired, Pete volunteers aboard the USS
Intrepid Museum in New York City where he
shares his experiences with visitors.

Have a book idea?

Contact us at:

info@mascotbooks.com | www.mascotbooks.com

For my aunt Daisy Byam, who encouraged my storytelling voice – G. H.

In loving memory of Spot and Herman – J. C.

This edition published in 2002 by August House LittleFolk,
P.O. Box 3223, Little Rock, Arkansas 72203
501.372.5450
http:/ /www.augusthouse.com

Edited, designed, and produced by Frances Lincoln Limited,
4 Torriano Mews, Torriano Avenue, London NW5 2RZ.

Library of Congress Cataloguing-in-Publication Data
available on request.
ISBN 0-87483-672-7
Set in Adobe Garamond semi-bold
Printed in Singapore
1 3 5 7 9 8 6 4 2

Sing Me a Story

Song-and-Dance Tales from the Caribbean

Grace Hallworth

Illustrated by John Clementson

AUGUST HOUSE
LittleFolk

LITTLE ROCK

FRANKFORD

Contents

Author's note

Once I was telling a classful of infants a folktale in which a song recurred throughout the story. The song words were preceded by the phrase, "And she sang …" I began to speak the words of the song and was immediately interrupted by a voice protesting, "But you aren't singing!" There was no melody provided, so I quickly borrowed the tune of a well-known nursery rhyme and the tale was transformed into an enjoyable shared experience, with everyone joining in the refrain.

During a regional festival, I shared the story "Dancing to the River" with a visiting infant school and was delighted when all the teachers and parents spontaneously joined in the dance. Teenage boys in Buffalo, New York, were equally keen to demonstrate their dancing talents only seconds after I told them them the story of a king who loved dancing so much, he invented a special dance – the Kokioko.

Most Caribbean folktales originally came from Africa, where storytelling often includes chanting and singing, acting out and dancing. Children enjoy the repetitive chants and songs: it gives them a chance to be "in the story."

I hope that these five stories will soon have children and grown-ups on their feet singing a story and dancing a tale.

Grace Hallworth

Glossary of Caribbean words

agouti	small wild animal hunted in Trinidad	*dasheen*	a root vegetable
		dey	there
arepa	a cornmeal pancake with spicy meat filling	*foreday*	the crack of dawn
		sapodilla	a small tropical fruit

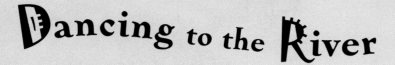Dancing to the River

Once upon a time and a very long time ago, the animals of the forest set out to look for food.

The birds flew high above the trees, searching.

The squirrels dug up all their hiding-places, searching.

The monkeys swung from tree to tree, searching.

Not far away was a field with plenty of corn. When the animals and birds heard about the field, they rushed off to find it.

Turtle was paddling in the river. She saw the birds flying off. They flapped their wings, klak! klak! klak! It was quiet in the forest and Turtle was lonely, so she decided to follow them.

Turtle made her way along until she came to the large field. There she saw her friends stuffing themselves with ripe corn.

The birds called to Turtle, "Go away, Turtle! Watchman will catch you."

Turtle said, "Don't worry about me. I'll keep a sharp look-out for Watchman." But once Turtle was in the field, the corn was too high for her to keep a look-out.

Suddenly, there was Watchman, standing with a stick in his hand. The birds flapped their wings and flew away, klak! klak! klak! leaving Turtle all alone.

"Aha!" said Watchman. "Here's one thief who won't get away." He grabbed Turtle and put her in his bag.

As Watchman walked across the field, he sang a calypso with such a lively tune that Turtle's feet just itched to dance.

Now, Turtle loved dancing more than anything. So when she heard Watchman singing, she called out. "Hey, Watchman, that's a real sweet calypso, man!"

"You like my song? I make up the words, you know," said Watchman.

"I make up songs too," said Turtle.

"Well, why don't you make up a song for me now?" asked Watchman.

Turtle said, "But when I sing, I like to dance, and I need plenty of space."

So Watchman took Turtle out of the bag and placed her on the ground.

Turtle began to sing. As she sang, she made movements with her feet.

She danced to the right
and she turned around,

she danced to the left
and she turned around,

she leaped and she danced,
she twirled and she pranced,
she was dancing to the river.

This is what Turtle sang:

Let's sing and dance to the tay-lay-lay,
Let's turn and prance to the tay-lay-lay.
Hear the music playing
And the steel pan drumming,
As we sing and we dance to the tay-lay-lay.

It was an easy tune to sing. It was a lively tune to dance to. Soon Watchman was dancing, too, shaking his shoulders and clicking his fingers.

He danced to the right and he turned around, he danced to the left and he turned around, he leaped and he danced, he twirled and he pranced, and he danced his way to the river.

Turtle danced faster and faster, and she took bigger and bigger steps.

Watchman tried hard to keep up with Turtle.

Turtle spun on her toes, she leaped and she twirled.

Watchman followed every spin and leap and twirl. He didn't notice where Turtle was heading, until he heard a loud SPLASH!

Turtle had dived into the river and swum away!

Turtle's Song

Let's sing and dance to the tay- lay- lay,   Let's

turn and prance to the tay - lay - lay.

Hear the mu-sic play- ing   And the steel pan drum-ming, As we

sing and we dance to the tay- lay- lay.

Turtle's Dance

R = Right, L = Left

The children stand in two facing rows, knees slightly bent, elbows bent at right angles to body. All movements are made to the counts given at the end of each line.

While song is sung for the first time

Let's sing and dance to the tay-lay-lay
Moving to R, twisting first heels together then toes together
(4 counts – heels, toes, heels, toes), flap hands from the wrist like fins, up and down.

Let's turn and prance to the tay-lay-lay
Repeat above, moving to L (4 counts).

Hear the mu-sic play-ing And the steel pan drum-ming
Rising on to toes, turn around lifting alternate feet, and end facing the other row again. Raise hands in the air, flapping them like fins (8 counts).

As we sing and we dance to the tay-lay-lay
With feet still and hands on thighs, make 2 small knee bends.
On last 3 notes slap thigh 3 times.

While song is sung for the second time

Lines 1, 2 & 3: Moving forward, and clicking fingers in time to the music, the facing lines cross and change places as follows:
With L toe touch R heel, then step forward on to L foot.
With R toe touch L heel, then step forward on to R foot. Repeat 8 times.

As we sing and we dance to the tay-lay-lay
Turn and repeat as before.

The rows of children are now facing each other as at the beginning of the dance, but on opposite sides.

The Mermaid's Rock

On the island of Jamaica there is a tall cliff and at the foot of the cliff is a large pool where women gather every day to wash their clothes. But at night the pool is deserted, an eerie place full of mystery and foreboding. No one visits the pool at night except the foolhardy, and those who don't know the legend …

Folk say that at the edge of the pool there once stood a rough, white rock. On moonlit nights it glowed with an unearthly light. This rock, they say, was the throne of a mermaid called Dora, who used to sit combing her long, silky, green-tinted hair, humming softly to herself.

The tune she hummed was beautiful, yet haunting too. And although the song had no words, to all who heard it the meaning was clear: it was a promise that what they most desired would be granted to them.

When Dora heard someone approaching, she would dive into the pool, leaving her comb on the rock. From under the water she would sing her song:

"Take my comb,
Return to your home
And I will come to you in your dream.
Take my comb,
Return to your home
And I will give you your heart's desire
Soo-oo-oooo-oon."

Not far from the pool lived a girl called Hazel. Her father was a rich man and Hazel had everything she desired … well, almost everything. For Hazel longed for hair that flowed down her back, hair that was as soft as the finest silk, hair that sparkled in the moonlight. She had tried everything – creams, oils, shampoos of all kinds, even garden herbs – all in vain. Sleeping and waking, she thought of nothing but long, silky hair. She spent nearly all her money travelling from one salon to another, from one city to another, from one continent to another, trying to find a magic treatment that would transform her hair and satisfy her longing.

Hazel knew the legend of the mermaid, but at first she didn't believe a word of it. However, after a while she thought to herself, "It can't do any harm to see whether the story is true." So one night she decided to walk to the pool.

As she approached, she heard the mermaid singing. Even as the sound chilled her to the bone, it captivated and drew her to the pool.

Dora heard footsteps and dived into the water, leaving the comb behind. The comb was so beautiful, it could only belong to a mermaid. Among its finely-carved teeth were a few silky strands of the mermaid's green-tinted hair.

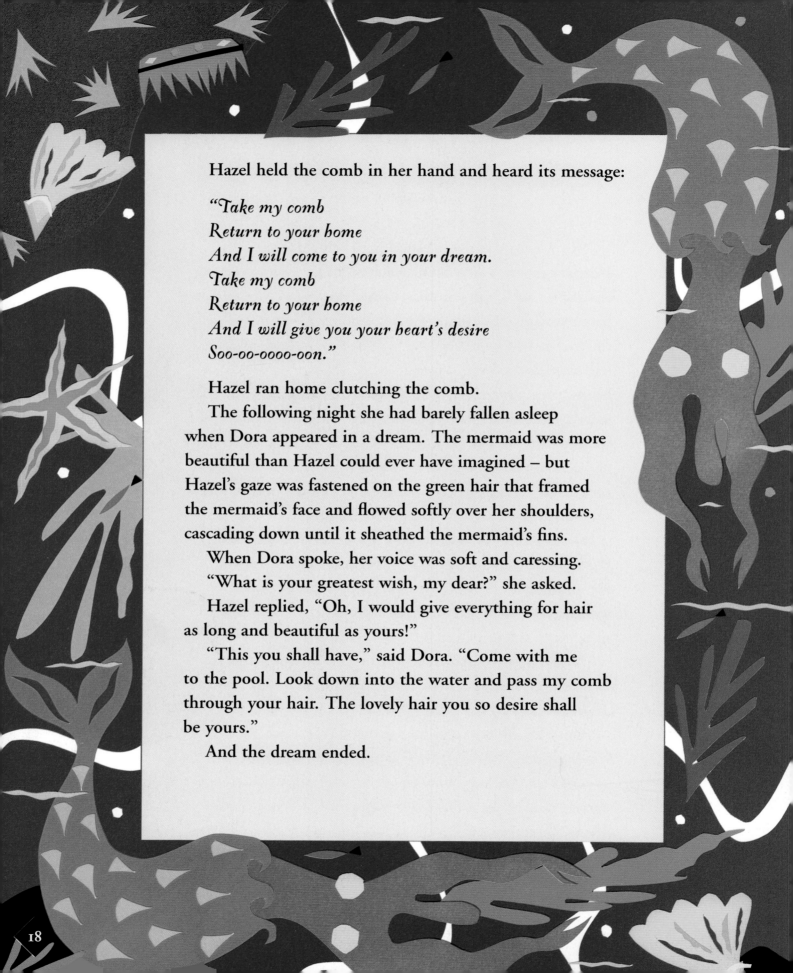

Hazel held the comb in her hand and heard its message:

"Take my comb
Return to your home
And I will come to you in your dream.
Take my comb
Return to your home
And I will give you your heart's desire
Soo-oo-oooo-oon."

Hazel ran home clutching the comb.

The following night she had barely fallen asleep when Dora appeared in a dream. The mermaid was more beautiful than Hazel could ever have imagined – but Hazel's gaze was fastened on the green hair that framed the mermaid's face and flowed softly over her shoulders, cascading down until it sheathed the mermaid's fins.

When Dora spoke, her voice was soft and caressing.

"What is your greatest wish, my dear?" she asked.

Hazel replied, "Oh, I would give everything for hair as long and beautiful as yours!"

"This you shall have," said Dora. "Come with me to the pool. Look down into the water and pass my comb through your hair. The lovely hair you so desire shall be yours."

And the dream ended.

Hazel awoke at once. There beside her was the mermaid's comb. She snatched it up and was out of bed in an instant, running to the pool.

When she got there, she scrambled up onto the rock and, looking down into the water, began to comb her hair. And each time she pulled the comb through, her hair was longer. Hazel saw that her hair now reached her neck, tickling it with such strangeness that she felt her blood curdle with cold. Soon her hair was flowing past her shoulders, and it was soft and brown like the tuft of hair at the end of an ear of full-grown corn. Soon it lay in thick tresses round her hips.

And now the rhythm of the combing became a command. "Comb! Comb! Comb!" As her hands obeyed, combing faster and faster, the hair grew longer and longer. As it grew, her neck bent towards the pool. She saw her hair spreading out on the surface of the water and, as it soaked up the water, it sank deeper and deeper, pulling Hazel, pulling, pulling.

Down, down, down, she bent until – SPLASH! The hair dragged her from the rock into the pool. Hazel tried to grab the rock, but her fingers slipped off its mossy green surface. She grasped at empty air and sank to the bottom.

Dora's Song

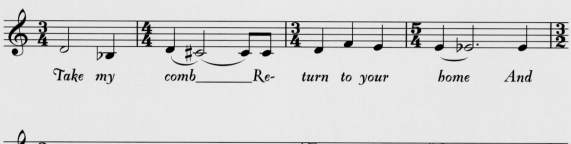

Take my   comb_____Re- turn to your   home   And

I will come   to   you   in   your   dream.   Take   my

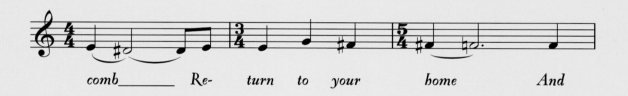

comb_____   Re-   turn   to   your   home   And

I will give you   your heart's de- sire   Soo-oo- oooo- oon.

Bouki Dances the Kokioko

There was once a king of Haiti who loved dancing more than anything else in the world. If he could, he would have invited dancers to perform for him every evening of the week; but he did not have enough money in his treasury to pay them.

One evening after dinner, when the king was sitting alone in his garden, he made up a song:

Kokioko, oh, Samba,
Now I dance, now I dance like this.
Samba, oh, Samba, ah.
Now I dance, now I dance like this.
Samba dance, Samba dance, Samba dance, Samba dance.

He sang it several times, then sniffed the soft night air and, swaying from side to side, he made up a dance to match his song:

Kokioko, oh, Samba,
Now I dance, now I dance like this.
Samba, oh, Samba, ah.
Now I dance, now I dance like this.
Samba dance, Samba dance, Samba dance, Samba dance.

And the more he whirled around, the more impressed he was with his own dance.

The next morning, the king announced that he would pay 5,000 gourdes to anyone who could dance the Kokioko.

That evening, a long line of dancers, many with newly-made amulets around their necks, waited outside the palace hoping to guess the steps of the Kokioko. And that night the king saw some of the most splendid dancing he had ever seen. But no one, amulet or no amulet, was able to guess the steps of the Kokioko.

The next night was the same, and the next. Sometimes by chance a dancer would do the first step of the Kokioko, and the king would sit up in excitement. Once, a dancer did the first and second parts of the Kokioko, but then he got the Samba dance wrong. But always, after the dancers and servants had gone home, the king would dance the Kokioko by himself, so he wouldn't forget it.

One evening Malice, the king's gardener, went back to the palace for his hat. As he came near the garden he heard the king singing:

Kokioko, oh, Samba,
Now I dance, now I dance like this ...

Malice crept up to the gate and saw the king dancing the Kokioko in the moonlight. He followed every movement with greedy, eager eyes and then ran home.

Before work the next morning, Malice went to see his friend Bouki.

"Bouki," he said, "we have been friends for many years, and now I am going to do something really great for you."

"Oh-oh," said Bouki. He knew Malice well enough to know that when Malice offered to help you … you were better off before than after he came along. No one was trickier than Malice.

"Bouki, do you know what I saw last night? I saw the king dancing the Kokioko. I watched every step. I can't dance it, because I am his servant and he would suspect me. But I will teach you the steps, and you can win the 5,000 gourdes."

Now 5,000 gourdes is a lot of money – especially for Bouki, who had many little Boukis to feed. And also for Malice – who had many little Malices.

"Show me the dance," said Bouki.

Malice sang and danced:

Kokioko, oh, Samba,
Now I dance, now I dance like this.
Samba, oh, Samba, ah.
Now I dance, now I dance like this.
Samba dance, Samba dance, Samba dance, Samba dance.

Then Bouki tried to follow Malice's movements:
  Koki-o-o-OH!
Bouki was so fat and awkward, he nearly fell over.

"Never mind," said Malice, "I'll be back tonight to teach you. We'll learn a little bit more every night."

Two weeks later, Bouki and Malice joined the line of dancers waiting outside the king's palace. When it was Bouki's turn, he went in alone and danced for the king.

Kokioko, oh, Samba,
Now I dance, now I dance like this …

There was no doubt about it: it was the Kokioko. The king was amazed, and had to give Bouki his reward. Bouki rushed joyously out of the palace with his sack of 5,000 gourdes.

"I've won, Malice, I've won!" Bouki shouted.

Bouki and Malice walked gaily home through the forest, but as they passed a large breadfruit tree, Malice suddenly said "Bouki, now that you can dance the Kokioko, I'm going to teach you a much easier dance."

Malice moved his rump back and forth, closed his eyes and chanted:

If you have no sense,
Put your sack on the ground
And dance.

"That's easy," said Bouki. He put his sack down and imitated Malice:

If you have no sense,
Put your sack on the ground
And dance.

"Good," said Malice. And he began to chant faster and faster and shake his whole body:

> *If you have no sense,*
> *Put your sack on the ground*
> *And dance.*

Bouki did the same. And his eyes were shut tight when Madame Malice crept out from behind the breadfruit tree, picked up his sack and carried it off.

Suddenly Bouki opened his eyes and looked on the ground. "My sack, Malice, my sack! Where is it?"

"Oh-oh – did you put it on the ground?" asked Malice.

"Yes, of course."

"Oh Bouki! I tried to warn you," said Malice. And he disappeared into the night, chanting:

> *If you have no sense,*
> *Put your sack on the ground*
> *And dance!*

The King of Haiti's Song

Ko-ki-o- ko oh, Sam-ba, Now I dance, now I dance like this.___ Ko- ki- o-

ko oh, Sam-ba, Now I dance, now I dance like this.___ Sam-

ba __ oh _____ Sam- ba, ah _____ Sam- ba

dance, Sam-ba dance, Sam- ba dance, Sam-ba dance, Sam- ba

dance, Sam-ba dance, Sam- ba dance. Sam- ba dance

The Kokioko

R = Right, L = Left, Up = on ball of foot, Hip = stick out hip to R or L.

The children stand in a line, facing front, feet together, knees slightly bent, hands holding on to hips, thumbs in front, rest of fingers to the back.

Ko-ki-o: Stand feet together

ko: Lift R foot and tap Up

oh: Lift R foot and place flat to R side (feet are now apart)

Sam-ba: Hip R, Hip L

Now: Place R foot Up next to L foot

I: Left foot Up

dance: R heel down

now I dance like this: As for ko oh Samba, but starting with L foot.

Repeat sequence from the top starting with L foot.

Sam-ba: Hip R, Hip L

oh————: Clap rhythm, hands at L shoulder level

Sam-ba: Hip R, Hip L

Ah————: Clap rhythm, hands at L shoulder level

Sam- ba dance: Step forward on to R foot, L foot Up to R heel, step forward on to R foot at the same time flicking L foot Up and out to the back, and 1 clap (on the word *dance*) at R shoulder level. Repeat step, stepping forward with L foot. Clap is at L shoulder level.

Travel step like this moving anywhere in the space, so that the original line formation is broken up, and finish facing front to start the Kokioko again.

Malice's Chant

See instructions for the Kokioko

TRAVEL STEP:

If you have no sense: As if carrying a large sack over L shoulder, 1 travel step on to R foot, body upright.

Put your sack on the ground: Placing L foot down and bending forward to put sack down.

And dance: Hip R, Hip L. Hands on hips.

Repeat as many times as required.

Quaka Raja

There was once a poor widow who lived in a hut at the edge of the forest with her four children. She loved her three daughters – Minnie Minnie, Minnie Bitana and Philambo – but did not care a wit for her son Quaka Raja.

Quaka Raja worked hard in the vegetable garden while his three sisters quarrelled and fought all day. They made fun of Quaka because he was kind to the birds and animals of the forest and always saved some of his food for them.

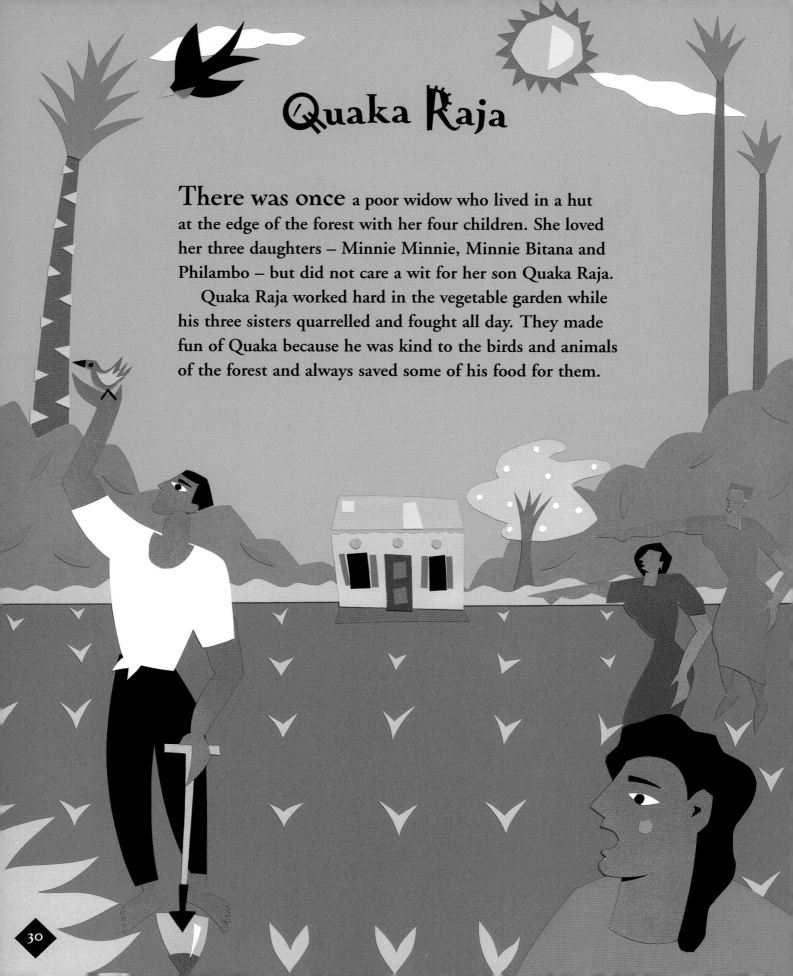

Every Friday the widow set out for the village market, where she sold the vegetables and fruit from her garden. Everyone flocked to buy her dasheen, yams, sweet potatoes, mangoes, sapodillas, peas and beans, and soon her basket was empty. With the money, she bought food to take home: arepa, molasses balls, cakes, black pudding and many other things besides.

When she returned to the little hut, she would stand outside and sing:

"Minnie Minnie, come here,
Minnie Bitana, come here,
Philambo, come here,
Leave Quaka Raja one dey."

As soon as her three daughters heard the song, they ran to unlock the door, pushing Quaka Raja aside. Then they shared out the food – and Quaka Raja's portion was always the smallest.

Now in the forest lived a man called Zobolak, who was feared by all the villagers. He was hideous, with a deeply scarred face, fiery red eyes, and claw-like hands and feet. Mothers warned their children to keep away from the forest, for whenever a child disappeared it was whispered that Zobolak had stolen it, though no one could prove this was true.

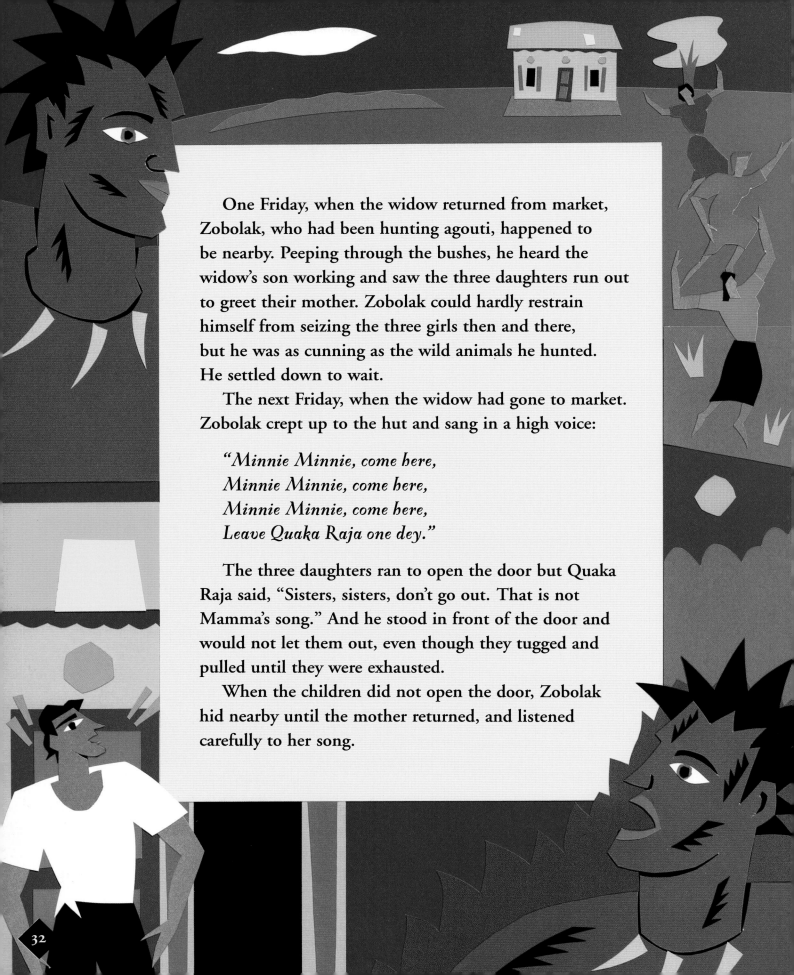

One Friday, when the widow returned from market, Zobolak, who had been hunting agouti, happened to be nearby. Peeping through the bushes, he heard the widow's son working and saw the three daughters run out to greet their mother. Zobolak could hardly restrain himself from seizing the three girls then and there, but he was as cunning as the wild animals he hunted. He settled down to wait.

The next Friday, when the widow had gone to market. Zobolak crept up to the hut and sang in a high voice:

"Minnie Minnie, come here,
Minnie Minnie, come here,
Minnie Minnie, come here,
Leave Quaka Raja one dey."

The three daughters ran to open the door but Quaka Raja said, "Sisters, sisters, don't go out. That is not Mamma's song." And he stood in front of the door and would not let them out, even though they tugged and pulled until they were exhausted.

When the children did not open the door, Zobolak hid nearby until the mother returned, and listened carefully to her song.

The following Friday, the mother set off once more, and Zobolak crept up to the hut and sang in a high voice:

"Minnie Minnie, come here,
Minnie Minnie, come here,
Philambo, come here,
Leave Quaka Raja one dey."

Once more the three daughters ran to unlock the door, but Quaka Raja said, "Sisters, sisters, don't go out. That is not Mamma's song." They tugged and pulled and scratched him, but he stood fast in front of the door, and at last they fell down exhausted.

Once more Zobolak crept away, but waited close by until their mother returned

At last Friday came. Zobolak's eyes gleamed with excitement as he waited. No sooner had the widow left, than he crept up to the hut and sang in a high voice:

"Minnie Minnie, come here,
Minnie Bitana, come here,
Philambo, come here,
Leave Quaka Raja one dey."

Quaka Raja stood in front of the door and begged his sisters not to go out. Their mother had just left, he told them, so how could she be back so soon? But they tugged and pulled and kicked so hard that he fell to the ground senseless.

Then they ran out to greet their mother, but – "Ayayayayay!" – there was Zobolak waiting for them. He threw them into his sack, slung it over his shoulder, and off he went to his den in the forest.

By the time Quaka Raja came to his senses, Zobolak was far away. Quaka Raja ran everywhere calling his sisters, but only the birds cheeped back at him.

When his mother returned from the village and he told her what had happened, she was wild with grief. But Quaka Raja said, "Don't cry, Mamma, I will go and look for my sisters and bring them back to you."

At first his mother begged him not to go. But Quaka Raja pleaded with her until she agreed. So she packed him some food and sent him off with tears in her eyes.

Quaka walked long and far. He walked all day, and as night fell he saw a light in the distance. Then he came to a hut half-hidden by trees and creepers. Inside he could hear his sisters crying.

What to do now? He could not rescue them without help. As he stood thinking, an owl hooted overhead.

At that moment he thought of a plan. He would ask his friends, the birds and animals of the forest, to help him.

Later that night, the stillness of the forest was shattered by a terrible noise. Zobolak was startled out of his sleep as the sounds grew louder and nearer, like the shrieks of a hundred demons. He rushed out of his hut and ran deep into the forest, over the mountains – anywhere to get away from that horrible noise.

What was the noise? It was owls hooting, frogs croaking, wild cats yowling, wild pigs snorting and grunting, parrots screaming and birds chirping and whistling. They had all come to help Quaka Raja.

So Quaka Raja returned home with his sisters, and his mother was so proud of him that if he wasn't such a sensible son, he would have been thoroughly spoiled.

And for all we know, Zobolak is still running!

The Widow's Song

Min-nie Min-nie, come here, Min-nie Bi- ta- na, come here, Phil- am-

bo, come here, Leave Qua- ka Ra- ja one dey.

Tiger Dances to Turtle's Tune

Tiger owned a large farm on which he grew fields full of crops.

At harvest time he needed help to reap the crops – but mean old Tiger didn't want to pay wages. So he visited each of his neighbors and said, "This Saturday my wife and I will be doing a big cook-out. There'll be wild meat, roasted yams and sweet potatoes and plenty to eat and drink, in exchange for a little help on the farm."

The neighbors knew what a sweet-hand cook Madame Tiger was. Of course they agreed to help – all except Turtle, who wasn't invited.

"Who needs a small, weak creature like Turtle?" declared Tiger when they reminded him that Turtle hadn't been invited.

Bad news travels fast. Turtle heard about the feast, and she heard what Tiger had said about her.

"We'll see about that," Turtle said to herself.

She went to see her good friend Armadillo and asked him to help her dig a tunnel alongside the road going from Tiger's farm to his house.

When Saturday came, Turtle waited in the tunnel.

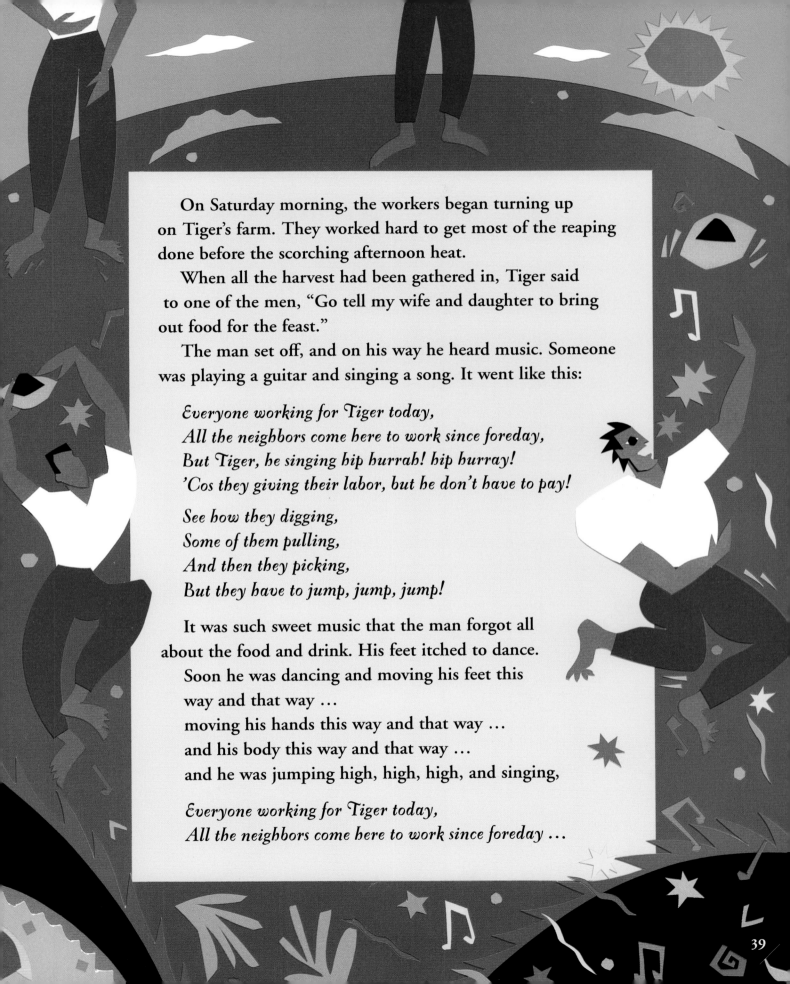

On Saturday morning, the workers began turning up on Tiger's farm. They worked hard to get most of the reaping done before the scorching afternoon heat.

When all the harvest had been gathered in, Tiger said to one of the men, "Go tell my wife and daughter to bring out food for the feast."

The man set off, and on his way he heard music. Someone was playing a guitar and singing a song. It went like this:

Everyone working for Tiger today,
All the neighbors come here to work since foreday,
But Tiger, he singing hip hurrah! hip hurray!
'Cos they giving their labor, but he don't have to pay!

See how they digging,
Some of them pulling,
And then they picking,
But they have to jump, jump, jump!

It was such sweet music that the man forgot all about the food and drink. His feet itched to dance. Soon he was dancing and moving his feet this way and that way …
moving his hands this way and that way …
and his body this way and that way …
and he was jumping high, high, high, and singing,

Everyone working for Tiger today,
All the neighbors come here to work since foreday …

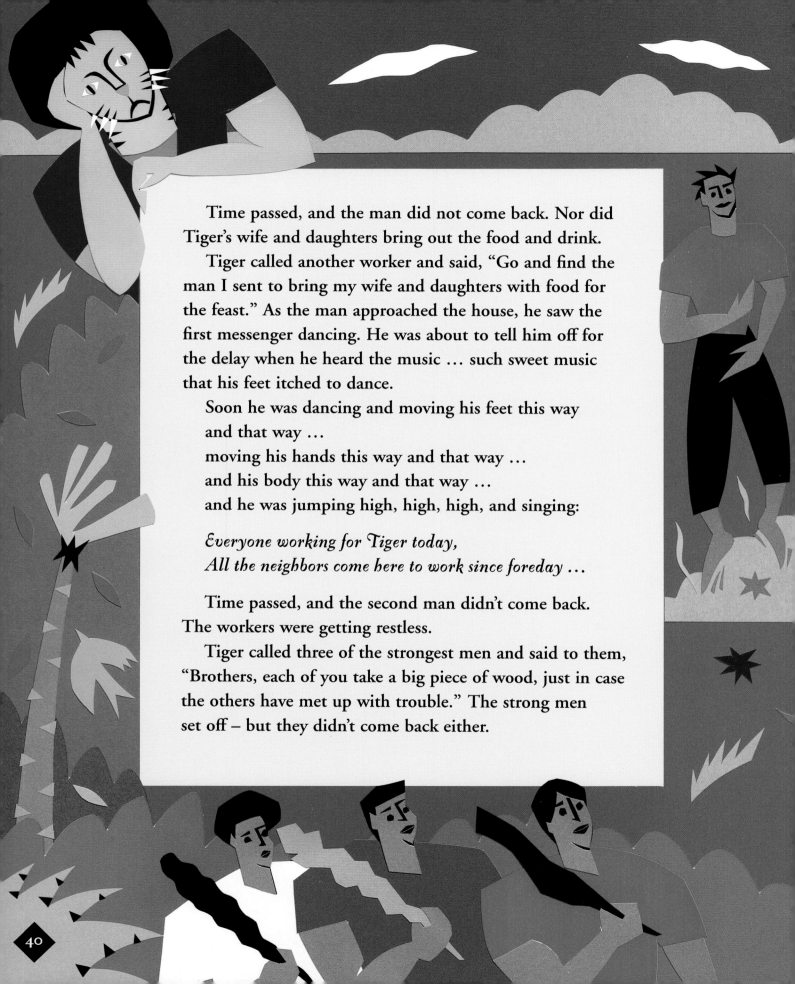

Time passed, and the man did not come back. Nor did Tiger's wife and daughters bring out the food and drink.

Tiger called another worker and said, "Go and find the man I sent to bring my wife and daughters with food for the feast." As the man approached the house, he saw the first messenger dancing. He was about to tell him off for the delay when he heard the music … such sweet music that his feet itched to dance.

Soon he was dancing and moving his feet this way and that way …
moving his hands this way and that way …
and his body this way and that way …
and he was jumping high, high, high, and singing:

Everyone working for Tiger today,
All the neighbors come here to work since foreday …

Time passed, and the second man didn't come back. The workers were getting restless.

Tiger called three of the strongest men and said to them, "Brothers, each of you take a big piece of wood, just in case the others have met up with trouble." The strong men set off – but they didn't come back either.

Meanwhile, Tiger's wife and daughters had set out with the food and drink. They were walking back along the road to the farm, when they heard music … such sweet music that their feet itched to dance. At once they put down their trays and began to dance.

Soon they were twisting their feet this way and that way … moving their hands this way and that way … and their bodies this way and that way … and they were jumping high, high, high, and singing:

Everyone working for Tiger today,
All the neighbors come here to work since foreday …

Tiger had waited long enough. He and the workers set out for the house. They had only gone a little way when they saw Madame Tiger, her daughters and the five men prancing and dancing.

Tiger was furious! But no sooner did he hear the music, such sweet music, than he and the workers all began to dance and sing:

Everyone working for Tiger today,
    All the neighbors come here to work since
            foreday …

41

Suddenly Tiger realized what he was singing — and stopped. The workers stopped too.

Then Turtle came up out of his tunnel.

"Turtle!" exclaimed Tiger. "Why you do this to me?"

"Tiger, I may be small and weak," said Turtle, "but I'm clever enough to get your workers to join *my* party, even though all I can give them is music."

Tiger was so ashamed that he invited Turtle to share the delicious meal his wife had prepared for the harvest celebration. And Turtle accepted the invitation, so there was not only food and drink, but sweet, sweet music to dance the day away!

Turtle's Tune

E- ve- ry- one work- ing for Ti- ger to- day,

All the neigh-bors come here to work since fore-day, But

Ti- ger, he sing-ing hip hur- rah! Hip hur-ray! 'Cos they

gi- ving their la- bor, but he don't have to pay!

See how they dig- ging, And some of them pul- ling,

And then they pick- ing, But they have to jump, jump, jump-jump!